For Katie and Zoë

First U.S. Edition

First published in 1991 by Andersen Press Ltd.

Library of Congress Cataloging-in-Publication Data

Ross, Tony.
A fairy tale / Tony Ross. — 1st ed.
     p.   cm.
     Summary: Young Bessie doesn't have much reason to believe in
fairies until she meets her strange and wonderful neighbor, Mrs.
Leaf.
     ISBN 0-316-75750-0
     [1. Friendship — Fiction.   2. Magic — Fiction.]   I. Title.
PZ7.R71992Fai 1992
[E] — dc20   91-4170

10 9 8 7 6 5 4 3 2 1

Color separations made in Switzerland by Photolitho AG,
Gossau, Zürich

Printed in Italy by Grafiche AZ, Verona

A FAIRY TALE

• TONY ROSS •

Little, Brown and Company
Boston   Toronto   London

THE CLOCK on the mill reflected four o'clock on the shiny roofs of Balaclava Street.

Over two hours to dinner, and Bessie was bored. Her book was silly — it was about fairies.

Fairies! They'd have more sense than to live round here, she thought, staring at the gloomy street outside. Why can't books be about *real* things instead of made-up things all the time? Outside, the rain was easing as a yellowy light tickled the black clouds. A long way off, a bird began to sing.

BESSIE went out into the yard and started to bounce a ball. Higher and higher, then too high altogether. The ball disappeared over the wall.

Scrambling onto the garbage can, Bessie peeped over the wall.

Next door's yard was just like her own, except everything was the other way round. Bessie clambered over. It felt strange, like going into a foreign country.

Suddenly, an old lady opened the back door. Bessie went white, then began to explain about the ball. The old lady smiled and asked when Bessie's mother got home.

"Ten past five, please, Miss."

"Come in for a while then." The old lady smiled. "My name's Mrs. Leaf, and I know you're Bessie."

AS THEY SAT down to buttered bread and cocoa, Bessie wondered how Mrs. Leaf knew her name. Then she explained about her silly books.

"So you don't believe in fairies?"

"No!" said Bessie. "There's no such thing as magic."

"Prove it," said Mrs. Leaf.

Bessie giggled. "You can't prove it. *You* prove there *is*."

Mrs. Leaf settled back. "Have you ever had a magic moment?" she asked. "A summer afternoon when the sky's so warm the world stops, or the night before Christmas, when you can *feel* the happiness in the air?"

" 'Course," breathed Bessie.

"There you are then!" Mrs. Leaf laughed. "Never pooh-pooh what you don't understand. . . . Why, even I might be a fairy."

AS THE NEXT DAY was Saturday, Bessie was given a
penny to spend, and she went round to Leach's
shop to buy some licorice. Mrs. Leaf was there,
chatting over the counter, so the two of them walked
home together.

"You were funny when you said you were a *fairy*."
Bessie giggled.

"Why?" asked Mrs. Leaf.

"Well, fairies are little, and pretty," said Bessie.

"They can be," muttered the old lady. "Then again,
they can look old and ugly. It all depends on how they
feel. When they're sad, they can look *awful,* yet when
they are happy, they become so dainty they almost
float through the air."

"If you really were a fairy then," said Bessie, "you'd be
a very sad one." As if to make up for her rudeness, she
added quickly, "Can we meet again tomorrow?"

"Of course." Mrs. Leaf smiled as she closed her front door.

"I'M GOING to pretend you're a fairy," said Bessie to Mrs. Leaf one day. They were walking down by the river. "Why do you live in a dirty old town like this?"

"I've always lived here," said Mrs. Leaf sadly. "You see, fairyworld is right here now, only you can't see it." She took a coin out of her bag. "It's as if you live on one side of this penny, and they live on the other. You're both there, but each can't see t'other."

They stopped by the bridge, and Mrs. Leaf pointed to the ground. "Fairies don't build anything, so in their world, there's grass right now where this pavement is." They walked on. "Sometimes a fairy can slip into your world, and if you are very lucky, you can see one. Only for an instant, though, and only out of the corner of your eye. Perhaps one day I slipped through, then couldn't find a way back."

"Go on!" said Bessie. Mrs. Leaf chuckled.

AT SCHOOL, Bessie asked her friends if they believed in fairies. In no time at all, she was the joke of the playground.

Of course no one believed in fairies. *What* an idea! With tears in her eyes, Bessie tried to avoid the other children, but it was impossible. They followed her everywhere, jumping about and laughing. After school, they even followed her home, across the field to Balaclava Street.

Wilfred Gosling flapped his arms, as if he were flying, and Edna Lord pretended to be a Christmas-tree fairy. With a lump rising in her throat, Bessie rushed into her house and slammed the door shut.

Why *couldn't* she believe what she wanted?

Why *couldn't* she ask what she wanted to know?

THAT EVENING, Bessie climbed up onto the hill above the town. From where she sat, she could see the roof of her house. She needed to think things out. She *knew* there were no fairies, because when her tooth had come out, her mother had told her to put it under her pillow so the tooth fairy could buy it. Sure enough, there had been a penny under her pillow the following morning, but Bessie knew it hadn't been left by a fairy, because later on, she found her tooth wrapped in tissue in her mother's treasure box.

But then Mrs. Leaf was not like other old ladies. She didn't get tired, for one thing. For another, she ate the queerest stuff. Tea and bread like anyone else, but she always used rainwater for tea, never tap water. She liked lots of lettuce and cucumber, never any meat, and everything was cold. In fact, she didn't have an oven in her kitchen. Sometimes she just picked wild berries off the bushes.

"YOU MUST NEVER eat wild berries," Mrs. Leaf warned Bessie one afternoon. "That's elfin food. You would get very ill if you did, just as fairies would get sick if they were to try to eat sweets." Bessie promised never to.

She went home by way of her uncle's house. She met him coming back from work, and after he'd washed and changed, he went to feed his pigeons.

"There ain't no such thing as fairies, is there, Uncle Harold?" she asked.

"Don't rightly know, dear," he said. "I've never seen one, but then I've never seen a pigeon look at a map, but they always gets home all right."

As she trudged home through the twilight, Bessie muttered to herself, "He didn't actually say there *wasn't*. Edna Lord doesn't know everything."

As the weeks turned to months, a strong friendship grew between Bessie and old Mrs. Leaf.

ON EASTER SUNDAY, the old lady was there to clap as Bessie walked past in the Sunday School Walk. It was so hot that the tar stuck to the soles of Bessie's new shoes. After the special lunch in the church hall, the two friends walked home together. They talked of the lovely day, and Bessie wished it would go on forever.

"If you *were* a fairy, you could *magic* it to go on forever," she said.

"Bless us, no, I couldn't." Mrs. Leaf beamed. "Fairies have no more magic than you do."

"What about the way they change from ugly to pretty then?" said Bessie quickly.

"That's not magic; that's just the way they're made," said Mrs. Leaf. "They think you big people are magic."

"*Us!*" gasped Bessie. "*Why?*"

"Well, you start life little and get bigger, no matter how you feel. That's magic to them. You see, it's only because they don't understand you."

AS THE MONTHS turned to years, Bessie left
school and started work at the mill. Mrs. Leaf
was still her best friend, although now that Bessie was
grown up, she called her by her first name, Daisy.

Only now and again did they talk of the old days
and of how Daisy used to try and make Bess believe
in fairies.

Funny thing is, Bess thought, Daisy doesn't look
a day older than when I first met her. Younger in
fact. . . .

Then Bess met Robert. He worked at the mill, too,
although not on a machine. He was in the main office.

ROBERT took to Daisy straight away and often said how like sisters she and Bess looked. In the spring, Bess and Robert were married, and they moved into Bess's old house in Balaclava Street.

Funny thing about the wedding, though: Daisy did not appear in any of the photographs. Sometimes there was a smudge where she should have been.

Robert laughed about that and said that something always went wrong with photographs if he had anything to do with it.

The three of them had some wonderful times. That summer, they even went to the seashore together. Daisy became almost like one of the family.

AFTER SIX HAPPY YEARS, it was announced on the radio that war had broken out. Robert decided to join the army. Bess didn't want him to, but he said it was only right and proper. There were tears at the station when Robert went off to London in his new uniform, and he promised to write. Bess was glad that Daisy was there to see her home; she felt so lost without Robert.

In the following months, lots of letters arrived, some from across the sea. Then suddenly they stopped, and the news came through that Robert would never be back. A medal arrived in the mail with Robert's name on it, but it didn't help. Bess was heartbroken, and Daisy looked after her every day.

As the years rolled by, the sadness about Robert turned into happy memories, just as Daisy had said it would.

AS BESS grew older, Daisy just seemed to grow younger. One Christmas night, Bess took a sly glance at her friend and couldn't help thinking how much nicer she was than the girl in the television show they were watching.

They still walk arm in arm along Balaclava Street, just like an old lady and a little girl of many years ago. It never occurs to Bess how pretty little Daisy looks. Maybe old friends never notice the changes in each other.

Now and again, though, a faint memory comes to old Bess. Something about fairies looking young and beautiful when they're happy. . . . Stuff and nonsense — she *knows* there are no such things. . . . She's always known.